CHRYSALIS: PASTORAL IN B MINOR

Susanna Rafart (1962) is a poet, novelist, dierist and translator. Her career as a poet began with *Pou de glaç* (2001, Carles Riba prize). Her other collections include *Baies* (2010), *L'ocell a la cendra* (2010), *La mà interior* (2011) and *La llum constant* (2012, Rosa Leveroni prize). In addition to her collections, Rafart has published anthologies and dramatic poems such as *Contracant* (2024), diaries, novels, and travel literature. Having been the resident poet at the Liceu theatre in Barcelona 2023–2024, Rafart has worked with numerous artists, producing a play based on Schubert's *Winterreise*. She continues to write and publish poetry.

Megan Berkobien is an educator, organizer and translator from Catalan and Spanish. She founded the Emerging Translators Collective, a collaborative micropress based on horizontal publication models for translators, at the University of Michigan, where she gained a PhD in Comparative Literature on co-translation.

María Cristina Hall is a Mexican-American poet and translator working between English, Spanish and Catalan. She has a doctorate in Political and Social Sciences from the Universidad Nacional Autónoma de México (UNAM) and holds a master's degree in translation from the Universitat Pompeu Fabra. She studied creative writing at Columbia University.

This translation has been published in Great Britain
by Fum d'Estampa Press Limited 2024
001

© Susanna Rafart i Corominas, 2015
English language translation © Megan Berkobien and María Cristina Hall, 2024
All rights reserved.

The moral rights of the author and translator have been asserted
Set in Minion Pro

Printed and bound in Great Britain by CMP UK Ltd.
A CIP catalogue record for this book is available from the British Library

ISBN: 978-1-913744-41-0

This book is sold subject to the condition that it shall not, by way of trade or otherwise, be lent, resold, hired out or otherwise circulated without the publisher's prior consent in any form of binding or cover other than that in which it is published and without a similar condition including this condition being imposed on the subsequent purchaser.

This work was translated with the help of a grant from the Institut Ramon Llull.

Catalan Language and Culture

CHRYSALIS: PASTORAL IN B MINOR

SUSANNA RAFART

Translated by

MEGAN BERKOBIEN

&

MARÍA CRISTINA HALL

And the days are not full enough
And the nights are not full enough
And life slips by like a field mouse
Not shaking the grass.
— Ezra Pound

Tot molt de pressa, amb molta agitació.
Quan el calze queda buit de mel i respira, la flor es mor.
I en neixen de noves. I vinga abelles!
— Mercé Rodoreda, *Flor de Mel*

Dramatis personae

The old man: Olivier
His wife: Emma
His son: Michel
Michel's cousin: Guillaume
The lovers: the young man and one of the
three young women Adèle, Maia or Cíntia
The tracker
The tracker's wife: Cécile
Cécile's dog
Pascal's wife: Cláudine
The florist
The woman from Bordeaux
The hornet
The forest
The chrysalis

I

THE OLD MAN.
THE TRACKER.
THE FOREST.

The old man had been expecting them for some time now, waiting in the shade of ash trees towering in their centuries. Scorching temperatures had completely dried out the grass in the sloping field behind their house. Suffocating heat streamed down and deceived the senses. One might even imagine that the old man — wearied as he was by his surroundings, staring out at the only possible road that the strangers could come down — was pressing his hands together in prayer. They were already late.

A bit farther off, at the land's edge where the ashes' gentle sweep gave way to a row of brittle pine, sat several abandoned hives, their covers strewn about on the ground. The old man remembered a time when he'd collected more than thirty jars of honey each year. Emma would label and arrange them carefully in the enormous larder of their country house — golden, dripping, thick. Touched by the memory, he hobbled toward the hives. The boxes were old, unusable, the bees driven out. He stood still.

The leaves of the ash trees, bone dry, intoned a few words. He didn't recognise the score, or rather, he'd forgotten it. He knew it began with a zephyr that meandered into brief stillness before breaking into various parts and harmonies. But what next? As a younger man, in the large house where he lay beside Emma, he'd matched their music by night. He'd held her, delicately, and entered her ever so slowly, attentive to each leaf as it brushed against the next, attentive to every turn. And he himself came on like the wind through the treetops, awaiting her notes of high pleasure when all the forest stirred. Then he would linger inside her. And afterward? It was useless to go poking around in the grey depths of his memory. The force of it all had never taken hold in the recesses of his mind, a force dulled by time, like those withered leaves, like that fleeting honey.

*

The tracker has visited four farms today alone. Out in the country, the tortuous roads often lack street signs, and your typical shock absorbers are no match for the pits and potholes. What's more, the data's erratic and no one really understands a thing. He has his work cut out for him.

First, he'd gone over to Bordeaux, and now that he's home, in the heart of Dordogne, he tries to peel back the layers. The *vespa velutina nigrithorax* landed in Aquitaine around six or seven years ago now. A mere thirty specimens can kill some thirty thousand native bees in just three hours. But you can't go telling people that their shipments weren't cleared beforehand. Some think it's a nefarious scheme on the part of Chinese producers; others take it as the collateral damage of unfettered global commerce. Its stinger is fine, far finer than the usual bee's, so it can inject much larger quantities of poison, over and over, brutally. Then it'll destroy the hive. Everything gets more complicated when farmers hide the evidence. For a second there, he seems to sense a jerk in the front wheel, yes, the right one. He needs to pull over.

It's punctured, he knew it. Right on that stretch of road with no shade in sight. It's noon, but the quick shadows of his feet sink into the earth. Needless to say he's sweating, and his shirt is soaked. He can hear a rumble from far off. An engine. Maybe they'll be able to help. He waits. It seems like they've pulled over close by. She kisses him violently. Their engine starts up again and they race by without a passing glance. Two young silhouettes burst out laughing in the face of his misfortune. They're beautiful — who could they be? The tracker sets down his spare tire in the middle of the road and sobs with utter abandon.

*

Crickets fill the forest with their wild orchestration. Daylight bears down on the fields like marble, exhausting the blackbirds still attempting to take flight. Captive to that same delirium, the ashes begin to see-saw, their branches full of dry, bursting laughter. All things seemingly come to a halt while the old man, his focus narrowed, raises his hands together in prayer and leans his arms from side to side, ever so slowly, just to keep his body upright, not a thought in his head. Maybe he's waiting for someone, but now he can't remember. In the despair of his forgetting, the only image to emerge is the chrysalis, clinging to the door of his library — a door he can no longer close because the larva has ensconced itself by the hinge, in the gap between the guest house's two worn-away, white beams. The sun beats down on the book spines, greedily drawing its tongue against the red tiles, forever cool in the repose of summer.

II

THE LOVERS.
THE TRACKER.
THE OLD MAN.

Do you still love me?
She coos and takes him by the nape of his neck, flashes a drawn-out smile. At the wheel, the young man frees up one of his hands and brushes her nipple with his fingertips. He's not sure if it's love, but desire courses through him. They've been driving down the sun-baked dirt for hours now, looking for a country house that's been passed down through the years. Silence. She grows tired of fondling him and slides back into her seat. Now she's zoning out, looking at the way the fields swell out into the distance on either side of the road, the hay already baled and piled into hefty cylinders. She remains in character — a woman in love — as she distractedly runs her hand under her skirt, sinking her fingers between her restless thighs. She's tired of this long trip. They've only stopped once, at an awful gas station where a man who'd just lost his job stole a pack of biscuits. That had really got to her. She looks at him. His nose is long and refined, and she can't stop fawning over his plump lips. She smiles at him again as she caresses her sex.

You don't love me anymore...
Then he slams on the brakes and desperately shoves his

tongue into her mouth. The sudden stop kicks up a cloud of dirt. Yes, he loves her, he's told her that a million times. She whispers something in his ear. Howling with laughter, they pick up speed. They pass a car on the side of the road. A man with a tire in hand stares as they pass by. When they leave him behind, he hurls his crowbar at the middle of the road.

See?

Satisfied, she thrusts her fingers back between her legs and closes her eyes.

*

The forest falls quiet at this hour. An enormous sphere hangs among the tallest branches. Two thousand hornets work tirelessly within. Feverish, their dark legs tear the common bees apart. The tracker goes back to his car to prepare the trap. He pulls out a bottle filled with wine and beer and pours it into an open container. Then, he places it in the hive. If he manages to drown them, he'll have won a small battle. He looks over his files; three more like this one in the area. He'll have to keep his cool. They're not aggressive toward humans, but things could go sideways. In Aquitaine, they'd decapitated half of the native bee populations already. There'd be no survivors if the bees themselves didn't react soon, as they had elsewhere. Some bees have taken to overheating the hornets, surrounding them with their vibrating bodies, pushing the temperature to over 45 degrees Celsius. But that's yet to happen here. He treads parched earth on his way back to the car. Sometimes he naps to wait out the heat. He always dreams that he's laying down inside a temple with towering columns, diabolical spheres hanging from above, spinning endlessly until they burst all around him. In this dream, he's afraid of falling prey to an attack, though his fear never materialises. He often wakes up to a light stinging in his eyes.

*

The old man drags his feet and pulls himself up the two steps to the parterre that leads to the library, separate from the main house. Inside that single-story building: a large table with books strewn about and an old computer. Beside it, the typewriter he's had forever; a few notebooks inked with sketches and notes; chairs placed around the wooden table, as if the man were expecting company. Dark-hued bookshelves filled with meticulously arranged volumes obscure the stone walls behind them. Here and there, a piece of cardboard holds the place where a book he's lent out once stood, or red stickers signal those books belonging to a set.

The man pulls out a volume chock full of illustrations — colour drawings of exotic insects. He's looking for one entry in particular: the northern hornet. It's lovely in appearance. He pores over other illustrations, too. Its queen is some four centimetres long and he can only make out a single, yellow stripe across the darkness of its fourth abdominal segment. The tips of its dark legs appear dipped in gold. He places his finger beside the drawing, for size. He can't remember what to call this insect in his own language. He can feel a stinging at the tip of his tongue, a murmur rising up to leave his lips, but it amounts to nothing. He surrenders into one of the chairs and looks around him, feeling desolate. Someone was supposed to come.

Painlessly, at the very least, he picks up a dictionary and starts translating, page by page, the lines of a text within his reach.

III

EMMA.
THE SMALL AIRCRAFT.
THE OLD MAN.

Emma stoops down to pull out the large roasting pan. She bends over cautiously; her knees have gotten the best of her as of late. She can hardly remember a summer as hot as this one, at least not since she and her husband moved here from Paris when he retired. You'll never get used to it, she thought, as she looked out at the staggering country house, its airy shutters and that large, ash-filled forest, a constant, baleful presence amid their rural solitude. But he'd swept her up with kisses and tenderness. Then came the beehives. Honey.

She ought to get back on her medicine before the guests arrive. She fills a glass with water and takes the painkillers. As she sets the glass down, she spies her own reflection in the window overlooking the garden. She hasn't aged badly despite the weight she's put on over the years. But she's no longer that carefree young woman from Place Vendôme. Time to prepare the duck. It never turns out quite right when Lucienne roasts it, even though she insists her recipe is much older. Her grandmother is from Lyon, so obviously the duck is prepared the proper way at home. She limps over and picks out a few potatoes from the basket underneath the stairs, plucks a bulb of garlic from the hanging bundle. A confit is no easy feat.

The duck legs have been marinating in fat for hours now. She readies them for the oven and figures out how long they need to cook on either side. In the meantime, she sits down and dices the potatoes to fry up in the fat.

Her knees won't let her go on living like before. She distracts herself by staring off into the distance. At the far end of the yard, she sees him lost in thought. He's standing in the doorway to the library, and he's likely no idea what to do next. He'll have forgotten the line he was about to translate, or he'll be waiting for her to come fetch him for lunch. Each day unfolds like all the others. She grabs a pan from the cupboard, arranges the potatoes and browns them. On to the minced garlic. His son, Michel, is coming this week. He's back for the papers, as if she didn't already know. Now then, she's gone a little overboard with the salt, but it's still missing the compote, a jarred one she bought at the market to save time. Their young guests won't tell the difference. She turns off the oven, it's almost done, and leaves it ready to go.

*

The aircraft hovers over the region. The high fire risk requires constant vigilance. Things that should remain hidden come unexpectedly into view. A row of elms — thin, pencil-traced — line the water's edge. The wooded area follows, then several houses and farms that have fallen victim to the infestation, plots among the fields, tractors and hedges. A stone's throw away from a hill covered in low-lying brush, fields of wheat. Back roads come together then part, a car on the hard shoulder, a man and a tire in the middle of the street. The aircraft tracks the road, another threshold, more houses and fields of varying crops, a car with its doors flung open, restless shadows dancing on the grass — surely they're going at it right this moment. On the other side, horses galloping in their pen, main roads, houses and neighbourhoods. Right there, yes, there's smoke, a signal. Alert all units on GR10. Fire.

*

Figa de coll de dama, a fig with thick skin and a long neck, yellow on the inside and intensely sweet; *figa sarrona*, bluish, only good for drying; *figa de la senyora*, very pink flesh; *figa del peçonet*, small and sweet. The old man sets down the dictionary and gazes at the wall in front of him. Volumes of Plutarch crowd a shelf tipping toward a door that's been left ajar. In the darkness, he senses the barred headboard of his parents' bed, the white sheets, the cold mattress, the books he's been arranging on the next wall over, those still in disarray on the mirrored wardrobe, and the door frame with its open shutters offering the prettiest view of the garden. He makes an effort: *figa de coll de dama*, the shutters, the wardrobe, his parents' bed, his frigid birth. He searches to no avail. None of it brings him pleasure. Groping around, he attempts to buttress himself on the furniture before walking out to the yard. He picks up a paperweight with several little houses inside it. He takes off his glasses, turns it over, and squints: Sant Miquel de Cuixà. It's always snowing inside this globe. Who brought it here? What does a *figa de coll de dama* smell of? He lets his gaze wander toward the main house. It must be around lunch time. Was anyone coming to get him?

IV

THE CHRYSALIS.
THE TRACKER.
THE OLD MAN.

The chrysalis summons the future. Its knowing eye negates all certainty. This is why the minor scale proves suitable. It's still pitch black, and the empty room expects the lovers to consummate their cycle. The chrysalis traces the young woman's silhouette across the bed, her pallor buffed by the bedspread's deathly ivory. It pictures her sleeping deeply. The mirror reflects a supple body and the dark hair of another strewn across the pillow. The chrysalis places the young, unpractised man there. It knows tomorrow everything will have been told, so it weaves desire into a still-absent identity.

It makes an effort — it mustn't tear what's been spun, tensing every mite of time within its centre — to make them come quickly. It imagines how it will pass:

Now the young man is overcome with desire to contemplate her sex. He kisses her there and wonders if she'll wake: there are books on these old shelves they've never opened. Sometimes, in the nude, before going to sleep, she'll stretch out her arm and pull one off the shelf

Read this to me.

Storytime can never stand in for the space of song. Like wild animals, they hesitate before moving but fall prey to their own curiosity. The chrysalis goes on:

The young man chooses a page:

> *And what life, what joy, lies beyond golden Aphrodite?*
> *I hope to die when occult loves are all the same*
> *to me, the sweet gifts and lair,*
> *everything kind that the flower of time holds*
> *for men and women; so quickly does wretched old age come,*
> *to make men ugly and rude at once,*
> *the boundless, vile angst consumes them,*
> *no longer thrilled at the sun's warming rays,*
> *children hate it, and women vex it, too;*
> *so terribly did God lay out old age.*

He thinks that, by her side, he'll never suffer such afflictions.
We won't grow old.

He looks at her again. Without waking her, he brings his fingers to her vulva, ever so sweetly, and grazes it. In her dream, she thinks a quiet zephyr must be cradling her in the grass. And then he pours himself ice-cold water from the pitcher, brings himself to her lips and delicately spills onto the kiss of her sex. In tandem they let out a moan the mirror won't reveal.

The chrysalis abides by the willing suspension of disbelief in its weave: Pastoral in B Minor. It renews its secret capsule, clinging harder to the doorframe. Outside, the buzzing fugue of night subsides, but the chrysalis must consider all threats. At some point, the warmth melts into its contained stillness.
    No, they'll never grow old.

✳

He pours the sugary liquid into an open container that he'll later hang from the tree. The hive is nearby, round and ample, a grey moon of papier mâché. He pictures the hornets buzzing and devouring other bees inside it. He'd blow it to bits if he could, but he's following protocol, this contract being his lifeline for the next forty-eight days. After that, it'll all be over. Cécile will ask him for child support, and he's two months behind on payments to his mother's nursing home already. Pascal is sick of him staying on. He's filled with the same rage as the fucking hornets destroying everything in their path. He's drowning — like them — as he falls. He's drowning after destroying everything around him, or more aptly, after building up the walls: Cécile's hate, his mother's indifference, his friend's reproaches. But he hasn't been systematic enough, not like the hornets, which rally around their queen, slowly surrounding her with vast, layered spheres to protect her in the hive, dynamiting native species. He's studied them, fascinated by their destructive powers. There are lots of ways to destroy things. He needs a drink, badly.

✳

He's spilled his soup on the table. He tries to collect it with his hands in vain, then lowers his eyes, expecting to be chided. Emma kisses him on the forehead. She refills the bowl with broth and the old man starts to slowly slurp.

Is there no more wine in the cellar?

Emma smiles and winks. She pours some red Bordeaux and takes the first sip. Her knees aren't hurting that much today after all. The duck is ready to be served, and she still has time for a game of solitaire. The old man amuses himself with the spoon. Emma thinks back on that time when they'd arrived home late at night. It was cold and the electricity had gone out.

We'll burn the roses.

What roses? It's winter.

The ones we'll be jealous of when we're old and grey.

He took her by the hips and, right there in the kitchen, made love to her in a coat impregnated with the scent of an enclosed garden. At the time, she thought that perhaps they'd made a baby, but it wasn't the case. It never was.

V

THE TRACKER.
THE OLD MAN.
CÉCILE'S DOG.

Look, ma'am, you should really be careful with the hornets. They're known to go after several native species. Butterflies, for one. There's no record of them doing so here, true, but once they've taken over their territory and debilitated the native bee population, how else do you expect they'll survive? They're predators, you know. And, worst-case scenario, they can be deadly to humans. I know what I'm talking about, really.

Anyhow, there's no reason to sound the alarm: it's only a problem for honey producers at the moment. No, no, it's not too serious, don't you worry about it, I'll set some traps and they'll be gone in a few days, you'll see. I've got it under control.

*

The old man's fallen asleep beneath the oak tree. When the sun spills over that very spot, the branches begin to bow, caressing the wrought iron patio table and chairs out on the grass — an improvised summer sitting room. Tired of waiting for their young guests, he's dozed off at the height of day, fool that he is.

The crickets' chirping comes to him in a kind of shapeless matter, like a metallic mesh surrounding the entire forest, barbed wire-like: when are we going home? He sees a boy dragging his bare feet up a sandy beach. A serious little thing, he's visibly cold as he trudges along. He wears a hat and an enormous scarf around his neck. Where'd he escape from? Where could he be going? Restless, the old man shifts in the seat that cradles him. He holds out his hand but the boy pulls back, not wanting to see him. He says something silly to make the boy laugh. That seems to get his attention and he cracks a half smile. Suddenly, a gust of sand erases the child, like a pencil drawing on delicate paper. The barbed wire closes in around him, gathering into an immense ball that rolls through the meadow with him inside. Then he hears his mother shouting: Olivier, lunch is ready!

*

The dog cheerily wags its tail. It chases after a butterfly, taking off down the street before suddenly changing direction, leaving behind a tuft of flattened grass. It brings its front paws right up to the pool of water. It sees its image in the puddle and drinks. The freshest of fresh water, and ever so sweet. It claws into the mud at the bottom. A large, black hornet floats near the edge. The dog lifts its head distractedly. A glass container hangs from a branch. It notices a trickle of that sweetness on its snout, a slick thread, reminiscent of blood. Refreshed, it takes off running toward the motorway once more. It doesn't stop until it comes across a pile of delicate fabric. Only then does it notice two bodies half-hidden in the wheatfield near the road. It's about to bark, but the girl, who's clutching the nape of the young man's neck, extends her snow-wisped arm and smiles.

Come here, handsome.

She lets out a slight moan, it approaches, head down. He moves in and out of her, absentmindedly. It draws a little closer, even though her eyes are closing. A tongue between her fingers. She glances at it and laughs, she cries and then laughs again, cries again. She lets her hand drop and open up like a lotus.

It hasn't the memory for sadness.

VI

THE TRACKER.
THE OLD MAN.
THE LOVERS.

How could Cécile do this to him? After almost fifteen years of marriage, she'd gotten everything she'd ever wanted. Two parts wine, one part beer, plus raspberry preserves. If this was all he had left, he'd say fuck it and gulp it down right then and there. But he has to keep it together, for the children's sake. He won't drink again — yesterday had been a slip-up. If it weren't for that couple . . . Sometimes you come across certain people that make you realise how useless you are, just to have it rubbed in your face. There he'd been, confronted with changing his tire, about to lose his job, fifteen years down the drain; and there they'd been, young, rich and carefree, casting him a look of blissful indifference — that is, if they saw him at all. And suddenly the concoction he's preparing for the hornets, the one he's constantly pouring and then hanging from branches and rooftops, finds its way to his mouth, and it sticks to his insides and he can't even scream, the whole thing's just so tacky, Cécile, the children, the two suitcases he's left at Pascal's place, his whore of a wife whose distrust is so unbearable, her robe half open — he could kill her.

*

The horses. It's always the horses. They gallop onto the page, kicking up words as they go. *One thousand horses with soldiers on their backs.* He makes an effort to translate one word into another, and when he's finally got the meaning, they come at him, their manes in wisps, and run off with the next. Old age is a pact one makes with life, replete with everyday humiliations. It had been a while since he'd accepted the fact that Emma had to dress him each morning, bring him his pills, take him to the bathroom. When they were younger, they were never apart either, but their contact was different now — body against body, so as not to fall; hand in hand, so as not to give up.

Drying magnolias — Emma's scent. A drugstore-like smell invades their space, permeating everything, imposing itself between their caresses, dripping onto the duck he once loved but now only likes. *Confit de canard.* It melts in the mouth. The horses won't stop their trot, day in and day out, tearing up pages he's already written. They storm into his mouth, grazing on his memory.

*

They're lost among the pathways and dirt roads and can't find the house.

What about a map?

They haven't got one. The car is too new — a whim of Adèle's. Maybe he shouldn't have listened to her, leaving so hastily, without a test drive first. Eight hundred kilometres and now they don't know which way to go. She twirls her hair in her fingers, questioning him with her eyes. It doesn't matter, they'll go that way. There's still time before dusk.

What about the old man? Wasn't the old man waiting for

them? A trace of impatience crosses her forehead. The field loses light, giving way to sleep as the sun cloaks itself in the whimsical folds of nightfall.

You'll like him.

And decidedly, as if knowing which way to go, he turns left, looking for a main road. Then he drives on, twists to the right once more and stops in front of a chapel.

We can't be that far.

She rests her palm on his hand, which grips the gear. There are no more clouds here. She thinks about the nights to come. They find themselves going in circles, driving past a small town, pressing on in the never-ending tunnel of desire. They no longer think the trip's been too long; brooding, they gather fantasies for later.

VII

THE OLD MAN.
THE HORNET.
THE SON.

The old man gathers juniper branches. Her eyes are grey, he knows that much, and she wears a silky, copper-coloured scarf. That's how the young must be — meticulous yet indifferent to how it all comes together. They've no time for heroism. How long will you be lying around, kids? He must go on waiting for them, attend to them, but they take their time. He starts to lose his balance and tries to grab hold of the trunk of the ash tree, but he fumbles and twigs fall to the ground below. He collapses on his seat, legs splayed out in front of him. The heroism of standing upright, of remaining attentive to the whole. Love is already old hat at that age.

Emma spots him from the kitchen. She drops everything and rushes over.

Olivier! Olivier! Are you alright?

She takes long, difficult strides through the dry grass. Her knees ache. The old man looks farther off at the patio between the library and main house and thinks that it's already too late to bring the two worlds together. A young woman comes into view: a kerchief, evanescent like the wash of twilight, hangs around her neck. They'll find him with his mouth agape, holding back tears: his body feels the pain of the fall, but the duck is ready to be served, Emma makes sure of that.

A man has every right to protect his land, wife and children; to refuse to take up arms for his country, to prefer the peace of his home and forget the outside world. An old man has every right to hide his humiliation from the eager eyes of the young, better he not answer for past mistakes. An old artist has every right to follow his heart's desire when beauty stands between the wall of years and the moth of feeling.

*

The hornet hovers among the water lilies. It draws near. The black spot parts the flower and its petals fall. There's one bluish buzz that fashions the air like a delicate blouse, while another unrelenting buzz bleats and blemishes the new shoots of the undergrowth. The dog pauses to track the insect, senses something amiss and then trots in small circles between the columbine and ferns, their hoarse moans betraying their thirst. One needn't always jump to action. It pulls back, stippling the grass beneath it, heading toward the car. The man's fallen asleep with the doors wide open. He has one of his sugary traps on the passenger seat. Hanging from the rear-view mirror are two snapshots of his children tied together with a yellow bow. He curls up between his muddied boots, snoring loudly. He smells of sex on the sly, of resignation, of churning rage — all roots and nails.

The hornet enters the receptacle, about to fall into the trap, but then retreats, planting its legs on the steering wheel before taking off, thick with the breath of that weathered mouth.

*

Olivier's son sits at the crossroads between the town and the country homes. A sports car had sped past him right as he went to turn. Music was blasting from the car's speakers, and the woman in the passenger seat was wrapped up in a scarf. It seemed like they were headed toward the house. He's thought it through. He remembers Emma on that first day: a pistachio-coloured dress, chatty, deep-red lips. His father's blue eyes. They'd wanted him to stay for lunch. Duck with cream of apple. They served it to him on his mother's dishware, Catalan crockery that'd been part of her dowry. The plates for serving meat were painted with glazed game birds, their edges rimmed in green.

They didn't belong to her, those plates didn't belong to her. He gestures with his head, looking back and then ahead, nervous-like, compulsive, not quite shaking it no. He takes off his glasses to clean the lenses, wiping them vigorously with a towelette. He mulls it over. It's his father's birthday. He starts the car and turns around.

Cousin Guillaume will be at the town bar. They'll drink until their hearts say when.

VIII

THE LOVERS.
THE OLD MAN.
THE CHRYSALIS.

How many years can a chrysalis survive?

The young woman asks Emma, who demonstrates how to open the shutters without endangering the pupa. It's clinging to a white, wooden beam, right on the frame, which is why she always leaves the door ajar. It would be a shame for it to get damaged. They've grown so scarce lately. It's dark out and Emma won't stop talking. She can barely see her.

Months, weeks . . . it depends.

Emma's voice is as velvety as a butterfly's wings, but the young woman turns to look at another velveteen texture in the dark room. She notices the light-coloured bedspread weighing down on the bed, the many books lining the wall. She feels a strange sense of familiarity, but she's too young to believe in the past. The closet mirror jiggles when they shut the window panes.

The bathhouse is outside. You'll have to cross the garden. I'll leave you two a lantern.

The woman drops her scarf to the floor and peels off her shoes. They've yet to turn on the lights. They appreciate this newfound darkness after such a long trip. He's exhausted, but she feels for him anyway. She grabs him by the waist and slowly unbuttons his white shirt, then his linen pants. The moon's snowy hues light up his body. Her cream-coloured dress slips to her feet. The chrysalis clings tightly to the world.

*

The old man is listening to the radio. A cut in the transmission wakes him up. Emma has dozed off. If he can muster the strength, he'll go out and take in the sky tonight. *La nuit des larmes de saint Laurent* — the night of the Perseid meteor shower. Memories flash by, quick as shooting stars. He recalls his neighbour, back when his father used to work in Lyon. He and his brother could always cook up a way to drive their mother crazy. She'd often kick them both out to the porch, hauling out a pair of suitcases and saying, "You better get going," shutting the door behind them. They'd be outside, crying for a while, not knowing what to do. The entire scene would play out frequently. One day, the neighbour stuck out his head: "Ma'am, leave them to me. I'll give them music lessons." His eyes were muddy and pale.

Now he's with his brother, by the window, holding a violin. He can't hear the melody, but he can picture his teacher's countenance, his infinite patience. *Grave.* Now there's Emma standing before a shop window. He still doesn't know her name's Emma. She asks him where the library is in Lyon. He still doesn't know the colour of her eyes. She smells so sweet. *The End.*

He sees himself walk slowly, but he slips down the slope. He doesn't know what's made him lose his balance. His mother covers his wound with the finest of handkerchiefs. *The radio transmission is back.* Spain to formally request a bailout. Two dead on the motorway. Northern hornet invasion control efforts. And now, *Harold Pinter*, the classic radio drama. He notices his pants are wet and cries, galloping across the Italian plains.

*

The somber fingers of night fondle the tips of the pinetrees, which cast their first shadows. Its moist tongue brushes the ash trees' branches, leaving a scant few drops on the abandoned beehives. Each blade of grass grows separately from the rest, and the stars contract like a woman's nipples. The serpent's changed skins and the hornet's nest makes haste. It is now the time of the chrysalis, the age of perfection. Ensconced in its chamber are two larvae, exchanging fluids, impregnated with their breath.

The two lovers breathe in sync. Their expensive, delicate clothing strewn across the tile floor, the silk still twisting at their feet. The spectres' rondeau in the mirror has been quiet for some time. A hip emerges from the sheets, a hand is lost, the most tender liquid passes mouth to mouth. All excess must be stored.

They're hidden in Lucretius's ancient branches, blind to the celestial body: the larvae must mature in silence.

The chrysalis nestles in its creative prerogative.

IX

THE OLD MAN.
EMMA.
THE SON.

The old man knows only that he must release it. *L'herba dels canonges*, lamb's lettuce. Here the author follows the order of the dictionary, where knowledge fails to correspond to experience. The old man has yet to discover this fact, but what good would it do him now that he's noticed just how much his fingers tremble? He clasps his hands together and sits in thought, his body swaying. The bulrush chair creaks beneath him as he moves. Old age is made up of just such sounds, morbid as they may be. So the rhythm of things comes to change, ever so simply.

In the herbarium of his mind grows an abundance of feltwort, among sage and horsetail. They pass into his language as he translates — roots, textures and all. But this list isn't saying much of anything to him, or to any reader. He reverses the order, swaps a few words. At the end of the day, they'll attribute it to his condition. He mustn't lose the continuous blue of the trodden herbs across the page. He hears the voice of dawn: someone's crossed the garden to use the bathhouse. On the other side of the door, a body of white mugwort shifts between the sheets, solitary. Bare feet, hyacinths on a southwesterly wind, the intimacy of a woman.

This he must release as well. His parents' bed, the dim part of his library, the lapse between pleasure and its memory.

He attunes his ear, picks up her quick breaths. The young woman draws her hands across her body, wise in how she handles the wait, well versed in conserving that warmth. No, no we won't be remembered for our heroic acts but for the love we've given freely. Lemon balm, basil, cinnamon, the exact makings of a melody. She appears to be laughing; she's discovered the space of contemplation in front of the vanity mirror. She hasn't the willpower to move from that seat. The chrysalis keeps her in that unexacting spot.

*

They could drum up a little conversation, don't you think?
Their young guests had held up dinner earlier that evening. The foie gras and duck had gone cold. She'd taken the seat across from Olivier. The mauve of her dress accentuated its plunging neckline. The young man, yes, the young man had been smiling, and he'd polished off his dinner. He had a good eye for wine, too, having served himself two pours from the 2009 harvest. Since the young woman preferred white, Emma had grabbed a bottle from the cellar, though she hadn't wanted to bring up one of the better ones. After all, who knew how long they'd be hosting them. The wall clock chimed as they ate. The pendulum carved into the silence, as did the knives. She explained what made the duck so special.

Another glass of wine?
Olivier, pulse fluttering, served her the white wine. As if he'd been revived. He pushed aside the pills she'd placed beside his silverware. And he began talking about ravens.

There are no ravens around here, love.

But he was insistent about the shadow of the ravens, about the doe, about the grave omen they boded. She was absorbed in his presence. Olivier grew more and more animated, clasping his hands again and swinging them from side to side.

I'm too old to argue. Über den schwarzen Winkel hasten.

But that poem isn't really about ravens, as it were; they should have come with us to the sitting room and chatted for a while. It's only polite. We're too tired, they'd said. Tired of what? Afterward, she'd had to calm Olivier down.

Come now, we'll read the newspaper.

Unemployment on the rise. A new Miró exhibition. *You remember Joan Miró, don't you, my love?* Several men with jackdaw heads have pecked at the Rondanini Pietà.

Emma pauses. Olivier fixes his gaze in the unfamiliar distance. Past the window he spies the fugitive lantern bobbing toward the library from across the nocturnal slope. A ploughed field.

*

He passes the bend in the road with his brights on, then pulls over by the firewood shed. He crushes the dry grass as he walks. He sees Emma inside, newspaper in hand. But not his father. He's just about to go in but stops short in front of the fig tree. *Figues de coll de dama*, the ones his mother had liked. He takes out his knife and gropes around in the dark, finding the branch heaviest with fruit. He severs it in one clean cut, releasing an intense pubic scent. It'll never bear fruit again. He climbs up the two steps to the pergola and rests his hand on the latch. On the other side, he catches a glimpse of the old sitting room. The garlic and onions hanging from the wooden staircase to the attic, the pantry cupboard ajar with the same green crockery stacked inside, the economical kitchen with the duck in an uncovered cooking dish and the oil and butter on a plate, slightly rancid. The table occupying the length of the room.

At the other end, the large, stone chimney. There aren't any photographs of her. The half-empty glasses and dirty plates are lost in the vanishing point of the door to the back, the one giving way to the garden that leads down to the library. He catches the scent of a young woman. He walks around the main house, he stumbles over the fallen branches, but nothing stirs. Then he slips toward the back of the guest house with the library. How strange, the shutter is open, there's light in the penumbra. A note? He strikes a match and sees it tacked onto the beam: "Be careful not to disturb the chrysalis. A butterfly might hatch one of these days. Thank you." Nonsense. He walks up to the windows.

At one point, he'd taken up in his grandparents' room, right after that first big row with his father. He hung a plumb-bob on the beam above his bed. An antique he'd found while rummaging through some old trunks. The June that his mother died. A sudden movement: they toss and turn and kick off the sheets. A shock of gin to the throat. He sees a young woman clinging tightly to her lover. He decides to go in. Unleash all his pent up rage. He lifts the latch carefully when the shelf by the door and all of the books it's holding suddenly thunder to the floor.

Boars, wild boars!

The man hurries back to his car, opening his mouth wide to devour the sex of night.

X

EMMA.
THE TRACKER.
THE LOVERS.

In any case, Emma no longer plans on roasting the poularde. She'd spoken with Marianne, who was fine with it. She just isn't in the mood, what with the damage to the fig tree and her crushed rose bushes. If it weren't for the fact that Marianne had to bring over the wine, she would've just stayed in bed. Olivier hasn't been right for days now; he shuts himself up in the library, detached. Afterward, he'll sit at the table but won't eat. Yesterday, while she was reading him the newspaper, she realised that he wasn't even listening. In fact, he shows no interest in the reality of the wider world. He frets over their young visitors, he stalks them, he awaits them. He looks on to see if things are going alright, and yesterday he wanted to know when the honey would be ready so he could give them a jar.

Despite all this, he barely sees them. Some mornings they come over for breakfast, both barely saying a word. Then they leave the door ajar behind them until about six in the evening. They practically haven't shared a single lunch together. Yesterday, the young woman made an attempt at simple conversation while they cleared the table. She asked about the chrysalis again. The hem of her dress was unstitched and her legs seemed to be covered in scratches. It wouldn't be so hard to mend after all. The young woman sat down in the armchair and pretended to read the newspaper headlines. Was she to understand this as a kindness?

There's no need to make us anything to eat tomorrow.

He courted her with the flashlight. The silver anklet against her skin was all that glittered in the dark.

*

He'd been notified about layoffs later this month. Things aren't going well; he has to go. It's not good for the kids to see him come home like this every night. They'd tried to help him, but enough's enough . . . he tries not to think about it.

It's alright, I get it.

He feels uneasy in that house anyway. They spend their evenings in a sitting room painted wall-to-wall blue. There's hardly any natural light and the sloppily-hung curtains sit at different heights, the fabric grey and faded. When Pascal and his wife fight, he prefers to go out to the yard. A reed bed separates the house from the hill that dips into the river — turbulent, venous. The waters rush in his head, echoing all the while as he sets the traps. He's had it.

He's had it with Claudine painting her nails around the house, with Pascal showing off with his friends, with Cécile calling to check if he's drinking again. In the end, he'll have to sell the car, since his job is up in two days. Just another bottle, then he'll give it up for good. He'll go back home. And he'll buy Cécile some flowers in Bergerac. She likes yellow roses.

*

The young woman lies in bed, wearing nothing but the copper-coloured scarf. The young man sits up and scans the bookshelf.

Shall I read you the poem about the ravens?

She listens on, moodily, while the jackdaws pass over the roof of the library and peck away at her desire. Her eyes are shadowed by a winter sea, but the young man is careful in his recitation.

It's not easy, you know? Über den schwarzen Winkel hasten / Am Mittag die Raben mit hartem Schrei.

Across the black nook the ravens hasten / At noonday with harsh cry,* she repeats after him, annoyed because he hadn't chased off the wild boar yesterday. She gets up and reads the note tacked to the door shutters.

Don't you feel like everyone here lives for the chrysalis?

She feels like having a bath, but the other day she found the old man in the bathhouse; he probably gets ready at that hour, and she wouldn't want to bother him. Besides, it's too hot. And she'd spotted a white marble sink in the library's powder room, so she asks him to fill a basin with water.

No one will see us.

He smiles at her mischievousness and loses interest in the book. He embraces her, crumpling the silky fabric that separates her body from his. He wants to lick her sex. He looks up at her and gives in with wild abandon. Sweat drips down his forehead but he's unable to escape the sweetness that exhausts him. The young woman pulls back, lost in thought. She opens the door and remains there, studying the cocoon. She doesn't touch it.

Come here.

The vertigo of the countryside at midday breaks against

* Georg Trakl's "The Ravens," in translation by Alexander Stillmark.

his temples. All of nature chatters, hurriedly pumping blood through its common heart, though stillness remains — arising from danger, from shadow. The young woman takes a few steps forward, toward the ash trees. The brief suggestion of her body hangs in one spot. She lifts her head, neck craning with the tension of expectation. The young man grabs the basin and pours the cold water over her breasts and back. She smooths the last of the liquid with her hands as if fashioning a dress over her flesh.

The brambles moan. Stems sharpen their thorns, a beastly thumping rises in the air. The young lovers bathe themselves again, then again. They stretch and shrink back from the sudden cold like milky caterpillars in an embrace.

Suddenly, a blackened cloud lets loose. The young ones retreat.

XI

THE OLD MAN.
THE LOVERS.
THE CHRYSALIS.

I'll call you Maia.

The young woman peers at the old man from the improvised vanity by the library door. He totters and drops his books on the floor more than once. She combs her hair like a prepubescent bride. Her whole being exudes Japanese plum. When she looks into the mirror, she sometimes sees a taciturn, experienced face melt away into the fading light; other times, she sees an impassive girl staring back at her. Then the old man stands up, takes her tresses in his shaky fingers and arranges them across her shoulders and the suggestion of her breasts.

Maia, the mountain girl.

The old man recounts the story of the Seven Sisters and tells her how, sooner or later, she'll give birth to Hermes. He lays out everything he thinks with his hands, which are strong and radiant. Then he draws near the young man, his profile sharp, and examines him.

Excuse me, I've been looking for this book.

And the man is back to his old self, teetering off, carrying the volume with both hands. The scent of ether scampers across the room. Blood must stain the sheets. But he isn't privy to all that. The text advances on the page, and he recalls the words, their searing heat, as he sets them down. He turns back for a few seconds. The couple lie in the master bed's careful equilibrium.

He has to seize that past victory, breathing new life into it day after day. He leaves the door ajar and sits down to work in the stillness of the library.

*

A certain weariness begins to fall over the young man. As she dozes he peruses the shelves for something to read. He regrets not having chased after the wild boars. An easy enough gesture in the cave of night. He leafs through a book: "Tiresias survived seven generations of mortal men." As dawn breaks, he feels the urge to coil around her.

The sheets still glisten. His hands seek her, unhurriedly — the bud of her breast, her sex. He breathes in her moist lichen and runs his fingers first across the groove of her iliac crest, then deep inside her. His warm tongue relays his wet fingers. He delights in this second habitat and notices the rising tension in his own member. His mouth lingers by her ear. Now it's he who's under her.

The plumb bob hanging from the ceiling swings. Like a letter off the press, he's seeing it in double: two coiled serpents. He lifts his arm to separate them but the young woman, no longer asleep, lovingly kisses his penis. He lets himself go.

*

The chrysalis consents to its own vulnerability, the interruptions, the passing of days. To manipulate reality is to play a game of mirrors, a standing-in of multiple, shifting bodies. Clinging to the shutter, there between the garden and the house, it captures the stills of love and aggression. An apt technique. Anything can shift in time, in separate units. But if one seeks to understand the poetic sense of existence, one must understand that history and subjectivity are inextricable, an unfragmented continuum. True knowing will only come with constant attention to both principles.

The chrysalis knows it must keep the lovers under such conditions, shielding them from the falling rubble of the characters around them.

XII

EMMA.
THE TRACKER.
THE SON.

She starts with the provisional cast-on stitch as she prepares to knit a runner for the coffee table — that way she won't have to think about her knee pain. Her joints ache more now that the weather's growing colder. She's going to have to bring Olivier a sweater if she doesn't want him catching a chill for two months like last winter. He's delirious whenever he's sick, but it wouldn't matter anyway — winter's a bore in this house. Once in a while Marianne drops by, as does Olivier's son or nephew, but their visits are always kept short, doing little to save them from the waning hours, quiet as they are, and old as *they* are, too. Especially now that she never really feels like making jam, that there's no honey to jar.

They'd found the first dead bees that spring and then the entire hive came down. She'll have to hide the brood boxes away in the ramshackle shed so he won't catch sight of them. And ask the gardener to stay mum. The Ministry of Agriculture sent them a letter saying that workers from the agency would come by to check in about the hornets and to let them do their work. But everything's already dead. Too little too late.

How different those evenings in Lyon had been. After

class, she'd go out for coffee with her friends along with the old philosophy professors and sometimes the young modiste who lived next door. They'd stay there late into the evening. Olivier would always say that the city wasn't made for old folks. But what about the country? Who would come help her when the wind blew and she had to pull the shutters closed or when the farm animals got spooked? She'd reached the point where she'd had to hide a revolver just in case they ever had another scare.

She didn't want to hear that the country was better, not again. But it was too late anyway. In those days, Olivier could convince you of anything. No, the only good thing about this country was the truffle, and too much of anything will make you lose your taste for it.

*

He's got an ingrown toenail on his left foot. The pain is only getting worse. Pascal says it's starting to turn green. He can still sell his car and pay off his debts. He'll pay them for the room and find another job. Hold your horses, his friend says, and Claudine sniggers under her breath. That witch would sleep with him — she's a real piece of work. But he's set on winning back Cécile and the kids.

In a moment of inertia, he jumps in the car and drives for the better part of an hour. He parks the car in the forest, behind the restricted area, and pulls out his files. He jots down the variations: two useless traps, one destroyed hive, vandalism within the protected area. He scribbles nervously while he thinks about the bar, the glass of wine, and then the next glass, and the next and the next and the next. Then he remembers the flowers. He flips his wallet open: twenty euros. He can still buy them. He drives back to the town, toward Bergerac.

All night long he'd dreamt of Cécile breaking into tears at the sight of the bouquet of roses. But now he's the one crying, resolved to put an end to this losing streak.

*

He's talked it over with his cousin, and he thinks it makes sense. His father hasn't been himself for a long time, so it's up to him to make arrangements, think about the country house, the documentation, the land. He'll have to wait for a day when Emma's out, at the market perhaps. As he prepares the bird lime to lather the wicker, he thinks about making him sign, simple as that. Bits of bark and rope are strewn across the ground. He enjoys hunting birds like this. He used to do it as a kid, hiding it all from his father, who couldn't stand to see the birds die. But his Grandpa could, so he'd go hunting with him. Quick to the chase. Guillaume had skill. If you can't stomach it, what are you doing out in the country?

He gets irritated by the faces Emma makes when he talks about such childhood memories. See, life's a hornet's nest. Every so often, he and Guillaume would pay the local strip clubs a visit. Some women will dry up before they know it. He bears them ill will. You've got to know how to take a joke, enjoy life's pleasures, do what needs to be done.

All the rest is bullshit.

XIII

THE LOVERS.
THE HORNET.
THE OLD MAN.

The armoire mirror scatters the room's shadows, majestically so. There are two half-empty glasses. The focus of their domain. The young lovers sleep. The plumb bob hangs from the rafter, the disorganised books splayed about. Every so often, the shutters beat against their frames, taken by the wind. The bedspread peeled like a barely discernible length of bark.

An ancient spectre glows in the doorway. It sets down a wicker basket full of thorny plants and cracks the door open to let in the fresh air. The young ones don't stir, not even at the sound of squeaking rats. The spectre takes care to drive them out while performing a speculum exam on the young woman. No, there is no birth to come. Afterward, it strips the bulbs of their thorns and distils a sticky concoction to anoint the dreamers. It speaks their dreams in double, Gemini: they both ride on horseback through a forest where black truffles grow ripe. They continue along a sandbank until they come across a bed of pebbles and frogs. They leave their horses behind and begin to plod through muddy ground, farther off, they wade through shallow waters, peeling jellyfish from their ankles. They see grey-skinned people with oars, walls with parapets.

The girl searches for the young man in her dreams. And

he, her. The spectre vanishes, leaving the headboard and foot of the bed full of nitrate.

※

It dallies among the lavender and orange blossoms in ever larger circles. It points its stinger toward the flowers and imbibes the nectar. The veil of mist weighs down on the late summer sky and the hornet comes and goes from the hive, sensing a downpour. It passes several umbels, their perfume overpowering. A group of bees are at work. Black, assured — it prepares to strike. It has already singled out a bee: one sting then another then another 'til it's dead. It carries the bee off toward the hive. They behead it, tear it apart, devour it. The rain falls in torrents, filling the ditches, dampening the branches of the ash trees. The ferns in the lath houses glisten, the wild clavellinas sip the chilly drops: serpentine voices of water seep through the grass and the roots await the claw of thirst in relief and delectation.

※

He attempts to put the nesting dolls back together without much luck. He leaves the figures on the table in disarray — heads rolling. Life is chaos, there's not much more anyone can do. He's flooded by sadness, its origins unknown.

He scans the volumes in his library with restless eyes. Several ancient tablets filled with oral epics sit on the shelves. Emma brought them home, tied up in a ribbon — his first gift from her. That much he remembers. But he can't remember what's driven him to sadness, not that. He gives the snowglobe a shake. White specks enclose their own detached clime between the room's four walls: there's nothing to find there either. The old man sits unblinking, frozen in time, arms at his sides.

He sees a bus, then himself carrying suitcases, people all around him waiting to go to Paris. Those were his school days: a weekend in Rouen with Marie, poems published in *Le guetteur*, his first classes at Marseille Academy, a bike ride to Arles with Guillaume's father, and his first few years here, when the library wasn't yet a library but his mother's sewing room instead. Sadness bears down on him like a wicker basket heavy with thorns. He ate very little when he was young, thinking that the food would pierce his belly. His mother was always crying and she'd had to take in all his trousers.

He falls asleep, dreams he's atop a marble slab, his death imminent — someone's left him behind to die. He sees his own difficult birth and doesn't cry; he watches a bit too attentively and forgets how to breathe. The icy surface unnerves him and he lets out a desperate cry. There is no going back, life must go on. He now understands this sadness, the weight of decision. He blinks then notices the stiffness of his body, the chill of the stone slabs, and realises he's fallen. He feels his forehead, his entire face: yes, there's a gash. And Emma, like always, is there to put him back together again.

XIV

THE OLD MAN.
THE FLORIST.
CÉCILE'S DOG.

The peach-stained sun rises along the path behind the forest of ash trees, its light swelling delicately along the countryside hill. The old man stands half naked between the main house and the library. He's just left the bathhouse and doesn't know where to head next. He can feel the morning air and he clasps his hands and brings them up to block the sun, creating a rhombus shape with his arms. A strange chill bites at him. Then he stares straight into the sun and the blinding light brings a few lines of poetry to mind: *Meanwhile let me make my way / And pick the berries from the woods / So I might extinguish my love for you.*

He knows Emma is also his motherland, and the thought of it calms him, but he looks around and can't recognise the place. He can't hear the buzzing that once filled the air, nor take in the clear scent of fern. He understands he'll no longer pick a thing from this godforsaken garden. There's nothing left but the memory of it, a large and draughty house, a few corners where he could touch himself if he weren't so old. He shrinks back.

He once took a trip to see a friend. He crossed the border and went south along the coast. Right as he was arriving, he had to weave through a town that seemed tacked onto the mountainside. He and his friend trekked up a mountain range where eagles roamed, and they sat down for a meal and read all afternoon long: *I understood the quiet ether / But never the words of men. / Raised by the melodies / Of a whispering forest / I learned to love / Among the blossoms. / In the arms of gods, I grew.* On the way back, they'd even climbed up the castle's ancient rock garden until they reached a stone platform — a tender shrub shooting up from its centre.

War is a fervid birth.

In dreams, he's seen it burn.

*

She likes yellow ones.

The store is well-stocked with white pots and twine. Yellow irises, daisies, carnations, orange blossom, twigs, primroses, eucalyptus leaves, petunias, lavender, pansies, ivy, orchids; there are posies but also bunches for larger vases, fabric ornaments, scented candles. And roses, naturally.

She shows off her store like a bride-to-be would her gifts at a shower. She's pretty, with green eyes and slightly broad shoulders. Ever since she moved here from Paris, things have gone well. People buy her flowers and she's made back her initial investment. The tracker takes pride in this success, in her happiness. He requests twelve stems of roses. Taking her time, the woman walks into the refrigerated room and rolls out a tub of yellow buds. She selects them one by one, looking each one over, occasionally shearing a thorn she may have missed. She arranges them on a white table.

The tracker peers at her sinuous arms as she turns her back and chooses a somewhat bucolic ribbon: white and beige squares. When she was younger, Cécile had skin as soft as hers, but she was no longer the same fresh-faced woman after giving birth. The florist now cuts an amber square of cellophane to accentuate the flowers' pale yellow. She wraps up the roses and seals the cellophane with a golden butterfly. Her every gesture makes the flowers more ethereal. He pulls out the twenty euros from his wallet, the last of his fortune, and offers up the bill with a tense smile, a mix of regret and firmness in his decision. The woman puts the bill away disinterestedly and chats for a while longer.

Okay, same time next month.

✻

The dog growls at the bucket. It's on guard before the eerie silence, the quiet seeping into the deep of things, so it stays outside, mouth agape. Its fur moist, its body stiff, a growl like sulphur — it grows wild. The stinger passes quickly, on the sly, but it's losing its habitual curiosity. There's a trap laid out ahead, proof of it being the forest's muted rumour, like a broken slab of marble. It brings its snout into the oak forest. Black. Truffle black. Chrysalis black.

XV

THE FLORIST.
THE SON.
THE LOVERS.

The florist walks into the cold storage room and inspects the latest flower delivery. Everything's as it should be. The shop window needs rearranging and the new flowerpots should go out on the sidewalk, alongside the flower beds and planters, in bold flashes of colour. Out front, she looks at the other florist's place across the street, the one who's always been there. Her plants are set out every which way. She doesn't seem to find joy in beautiful things. But they're not in each other's way. Her own clients are from out of town, like the man from Mussidan who comes on the same day, at the same time, every year to buy flowers for his wife. She can remember how, when she'd just opened the shop, he came in and bought a bunch of yellow roses. And the next year, the same thing.

What a lovely woman you are!

One time, she could tell he was a little drunk, but he always behaved himself and asked how things were going at the shop. Everything's so different from how it was in Paris, since she'd left him. Here she works only with flowers, and that's more than enough for her: flowers and her customers. She never lets on but she keeps track of their comings and goings: the man from Mussidan, a little dejected, yellow roses; the lady from the local dairy, pots of hydrangeas and geraniums, when in bloom; Pascal, Claudine's husband, mint and lavender, for their sunny terrace overlooking the river; the old professor, the second of September and the ninth of February, a posy of orchids and lilies, and a bunch of roses, the first being for his wife, the other, not her concern.

The loyalty of her customers moves her, and she never stops thinking about new arrangements that might suit their particular tastes. For example, she'd just acquired some ceramic bees to tuck inside the cellophane wrap enveloping each spray of flowers. She has them brought in from Bordeaux: silk cord; jute twine; tangled ribbon; plain ribbon; several darling, ready-made bows; pom-poms to tie in.

It's getting late. She's been waiting for this moment. She'll put away the plants, the gift items; bring the little doorbells in; lower the gate and turn off the light; place the rocking chair in the centre of the shop, unbutton her blouse and let the scent of flowers seep into her skin. She'll even fall asleep there, half afraid that someone might find her like that, half fantasising that some customer might urgently need an enormous bouquet.

*

This week at the latest. The banks have him going around in circles, and money in the bank does him little good. He needs it.

Another, sweetheart.

He likes visiting this bar on market days. Folks from around the region go there to catch up, and you can always barter for something. The old man selling truffles won't be making any sales today, you can see it on his face, but he'll play along anyway. He'd better make something, anything at all really. The tobacco they'd confiscated had cost Michel business, the laws leaving barely any wiggle room — he has to be careful. If his old man agrees to go along with it, to give him what he wants, then it'll all be so much easier. He doesn't plan on bothering him or his wife, but there's no messing around with this kind of thing. He'd already let them get away with it for too long, and his mother also had a right to part of the estate.

At least half of the land, from the forest to the creek, and the money they'd used up on the first renovation. He has no reason to believe that they're *not* planning to leave him something, true, but he wants it now, before it's too late. He has an uneasy feeling, those young strangers . . . he's just not sure. How come they've stayed for so long? Guillaume had even said: "They could be family; they live like kings over there, and it doesn't seem like they're leaving anytime soon." Could he be right? He obviously won't ask who they are, but the whole thing annoys the hell out of him.

*

An outstretched arm languishes atop the sheets, part of it hanging off the bed. An unfurled hand listlessly holds a branch of blackthorn. The plumb bob hanging from the rafter assesses its depth: the string, the weight, the bodies. At the same time, nothing explains the bluish sheen across the room, the crushing silence, the wear and tear of certain objects like the yellowing scarf, the chest of drawers and its forgotten hair combs. The light braiding in from the library.

The shutter bangs against its frame, letting through the light in fits and starts. The hand remains there, unmoving, and it's as if a sudden gust could steal away with its fruits. The young man, like an unexpected guest, holds out his hand waiting for a move. It never comes. A quiver belt has left its mark on the skin of his broad, well-defined torso.

An archeology of love, the measuring device concludes.

XVI

THE OLD MAN.
THE FLORIST.
GUILLAUME.

The fig tree has spread across both sides of the library's shingled roof. It's all on the brink of ruin. He'll have to ask Guillaume to come over and have a look before the water ruins his books. Devastation arrives from the south: the fig trees of etymology, figs given in benediction — the foundations and rooftops wrecked by its branches are an age-old story.

All things exotic exact a price. But he can't remember the name of it. No, he'll have to call Guillaume and ask how much he'd charge to cut down the tree. Guillaume's own father used to do it, until the inheritance put a wedge between them. Staring up at the beams, he senses such tensions. It's too late to fix anything or make up for lost time. He'd stepped off one train to bury his first wife. He'd exited another to find a second. Only the flowers he'd buy them had kept him going. That's why he'd go see the florist so often: he'd either buy a posy of orchids and lilies or a bouquet of roses.

He can't bring himself to ask Emma to drive him to Bergerac. His memory is an anvil: hammered, tapped and hit until every single memory burns red hot. Then he makes himself an urn for the ashes.

He observes the tomes on the wall. Those books were once

his lifeblood, but now he can't understand what it is they're doing there. He feels the urge to buy flowers, to throw out all the books and line his shelves with roses, cyclamens, lush goldenrods.

If only he could bring back that scent. He looks for her. They're over there. It's been quiet for a while now. He cracks the door and peers inside. The young man's forehead gleams with beads of sweat that rain crystal in the light. She tempts him to nibble her breasts. But it's not her breasts that the old man's lost in. It's the young man's decisiveness, his fearless tongue, his hands not hesitating, his elbows, so white and firm, flexed in the game of love.

She stops him. The young couple freezes like basalt. The woman has discovered the old man. But she smiles at him in consent. She peels back the sheet and draws the young man's penis toward her, tracing it with her fingers in deep surrender. She straddles him. Now it's the young woman's blue skin barely reflected in the mirror, like a sigh. She stands up, relishing it all — the old man's feebleness like a strange tingling at the base of her spine.

Maia.

Her tattoo quivers in the mirror. Still, despite the shock of seeing the old man, she strokes her lover until he clings to her. Everything is born. The branch that's grown against the outside wall finally breaks through. Light rushes in, a zenith.

✳

Her ideal landscape. While rocking in her chair, she takes inventory of the roses of Alexandria against the white linen; the pungent Damask rose; the stinging thorns and pale green leaves guarding the pink petals; the wild buds, crowded and sweet; the broad plane leaves fastening the ceremony bouquets; the decorative roots; the purple bunches of peonies; the daisies' lilac ligula; the majestic chrysanthemums.

The florist unbuttons her shirt completely, letting their essences seep into her pores. Then she mentally tallies up the ounces of cinnamon, the lemon verbena mist and the seedling pots of basil. According to her notes, clients come in between ten o'clock and noon on Sundays: the car mechanic only buys flowers after fighting with his partner; the woman at the haberdashery browses plenty but never buys a thing; and ever since he became ill and can no longer come by himself, Emma buys quaint, little bouquets for the retired translator.

At the table, she skims through her notebook and sighs. According to her records, Claudine's husband should be dropping by today. It's almost closing time, but a sweet lethargy keeps her from bringing in the signs and pots from outside. What's the rush? She lets the afternoon go by as she naps amid her curated plot of nature, a rose like any other. Caught between wake and sleep, a sudden uproar pulls her back to consciousness.

The tracker rings the bell violently and storms inside the shop. He's got a wild look to him, unhinged, with bloodshot eyes, shaking hands, scuffed-up skin.

She didn't want the roses.

He drops to his knees in front of her; she's not afraid of him. She wraps him in a maternal embrace and the tracker abandons himself in her arms, drunk on the scent of fennel she exudes. They spend hours like that — two people meeting halfway on a train platform — until she covers him with linen and hedges her mouth against his in her fairytale garden. They can hear a speech trailing in the distance, music and commotion.

Let's go see.

The florist stows away her notebook. They quickly pull on their clothes but leave their underwear behind. Exhilarated by that secret, youthful freedom, they join in the celebrations in the town square.

They see groups of young people, some laying out on the grass and smoking; little booths with pamphlets demanding the release of Basque prisoners; people handing out stickers; fire pits for roasting meat; Muslim families with kids and baskets full of food, somewhat apart from the rest. A heavy, round moon rises above the park, and the speech comes to an end. Later on, the thunder of protesters dies down, a flag burns.

The florist and the tracker sit in a corner, surprised at their own brazenness. They chat discreetly, feeling for each other between smiles like they've happened upon some forbidden place.

*

Guillaume prepares his tools as he sets out to fix the shingles. He'll have to work carefully. The roof is quite steep, and nobody's done any repairs for quite some time. He cares deeply for his uncle. Michel wants to develop the land into a housing estate; people have to keep up with the times, and the future holds plenty of opportunity. His uncle won't come around so easily.

Guillaume hesitates to argue with him. He's always respected his uncle, and when he'd run out of his own father's money, his uncle had helped him set up a bar. No, he can't bring himself to betray him. He sets the shingles tightly, one atop the other. He takes in all the spaces from his childhood:

the main house, the granary where he would dissect birds with Michel, the library with his grandparents' dark room, always shut, the sloping field fenced off by ash trees above and by pine trees on the far side — though now that it's autumn and their needles have fallen, onlookers can see right through.

One day, they'd pried open the hives as a prank and were stung from head to toe. Emma was furious, but Uncle Olivier spent two days dressing their wounds. He'd tell them about the legend of Jean de l'Ours — the hairy cave-child who'd swing from the battlements of bell towers. Uncle never saw eye to eye with Michel, and ever since *she's* been there, it's like there's a chasm between them. But that didn't warrant them tricking him into signing off on a tourist complex.

There are just a few shingles left. The crack went on for quite a ways, but nothing's ruined, no. He won't mention any of Michel's plans to his uncle. He covers it all up, not realising that there's ivy rooted on the other side.

XVII

THE NARRATOR.
CÉCILE.
THE LOVERS.

The neighbourhood lies within Dordogne, spanning several kilometres to the north of Bergerac, with a scant six families still living there. Cécile's parents are sharecroppers on one of the more inconspicuous properties. Guillaume inherited a large part of his parents' land, which he then had to sell to his uncle in order to save his bar. Now he only owns the house abutting the ice cellar near the motorway. That's all family land, and Olivier's own family lives on a lovely country estate that's kept the spirit of bygone times, right near the village church.

Pascal and Claudine, meanwhile, bought the fields and house bordering the river with a mortgage. The rest has ended up in the hands of outsiders who spend their summers here but very little else. One way or another, the tracker, Michel, the florist and the dog cross these places at their own risk, captured by their provincial ancestors time and again.

Nature has recorded neither the hatreds nor the passions that drive their actions, eliciting readers' judgement in turn. The millet, plovers, hornets, river and chrysalis are multiform agents in their inability to access the symbolic world. *Before* and *after* are constant in their error, in their struggle to claim dominion over a time beyond their own.

*

Claudine was nowhere to be found when Cécile collected the children from school. Still simmering, she'll have to wait to tell her all about that rage she felt at his showing up with yellow roses. He was drunk off his ass. What else was she to do? Their youngest was crying, what with his constant ear infections. She can't take it anymore. Then the doorbell rang. She couldn't believe it — her husband. He looked fine, but then she smelled it on him. Just like always. He wanted to come in.

Don't you remember, honey?

She'd done her best. And their son in tears. She had to kick him out, for herself and for the kids. And the flowers, too.

Find some other woman.

She saw him stumbling over to the plaza. Mrs. Emma was walking by with a basket on her arm. It didn't take him two seconds to hand over the flowers. *Her* flowers. Yes, she'd really watched him do that. Then her oldest cracked his head on the table and she'd had to run out to the pharmacy. Like always.

Do you need anything, darling?

Emma was tickled pink over that bouquet of flowers meant for her. What would she do with them? What was an old woman to do with such flowers? As her child's blood ran down her arms, she cursed the day she'd left home to marry that bastard.

*

The young lovers have learned there are no creatures droning outside. Wrapped up in the sheets, they contemplate the plumb bob above their heads. A layer of grey air circles the room but they're not the least bit cold. In the library, the old man sings: *when it all died down, the trees resembled crosses.* They stretch out their arms, hand over hand, and resemble a cross. It's not that they're complaining about the gesture he forces them to make with his words, but rather that they must do so with the same resoluteness they lend to their acts of love.

That was the deal, right?

Armed with a kiss, they go round in circles until they give in to exhausted abandon. The hanging plumb bob swings slightly toward the garden gate and then back to its central position. It's a bit windy, they notice, but no matter. If all is one, there's no need to guard against anything. With a taste for seduction, the young woman retrieves the copper-coloured scarf, grown sallow in the shadows, and veils her face, awaiting her lover's lips. Taste of spider, wild flowers, vinegar-laced autumn eve.

XVIII

THE OLD MAN.
THE LOVERS.
CÉCILE'S DOG.

The shooting arrow stills. The old man turns the snow globe upside down. So, too, stills the falling snow. As do the lovers in the bedroom. He can't grasp what's happening — how might he gather all these possibilities within a single context? He stares at the freshly repaired ceiling. Guillaume's workmanship.

A fog blurs his prior thought's precision and he nods off. In his dream, a throng of people clamour in unison. Red and yellow ribbons flutter from the branches, grazing the tree bark and just skimming the heads of the unmoving crowd below. The multitude slowly climbs over a great, solid wall. They make it to the other side, covered in dirt from the rubble — some of them fall to the ground. The old man's hoarse cry directs them toward a clearing but a curtain of sandy wind keeps him from seeing what comes next. He can feel the arrow pulling toward his heart, suddenly struck still.

So, shall we stay in today?

Emma prods him with a serving spoon, pressing him to try the onion soup she made with Marianne's recipe.

※

He sometimes wishes she had green eyes, and other times he wishes they were grey. The young man watches her sleep. He plays with her hair, pulls it into a moustache, then leaves her half bald.

Cíntia.

She won't stir. Their car drives calmly along the endless path of newly planted plane trees dividing La Roque-Gageac from Lalinde. He remembers. She promises to dress as a man once they reach the inn. They stop at a marketplace in an arcade.

It's quite small, just six or seven vendors peddling marmalade, tomatoes, cheese, truffles . . . Wisteria clings to the columns and everything looks ripe, mature, even — the produce, the arcade, the square. He remembers.

There's a little restaurant right beside the market. They eat mushrooms in a white wine reduction. She's blonde now, and light-hearted. They play footsie. As they finish up their coffee, he shows her his closed fist. Then he opens it: a few pilfered grapes. It's been a long trip. They stop by the river, its waters churning and kicking up foam. She's lost in thought, her eyes black — true black. He runs his fingers across her forehead and a furrow remains. Like the stone recess of a Roman doorway, like the Abbey at Moissac. If only for a moment.

She lets out a laugh, and as they follow the sandy paths, they come upon a Templar chapel. Improvidently wild, its enigma heightens at sundown; now Cíntia's black hair braids with the evening air. He remembers. He can't bring himself to stop the car when they see a flustered man by the side of the road.

Cíntia.

He opens up a book and grabs an apple. There's only this. As she sleeps, he places the apple in her hand, which hangs off the side of the bed. How he'd fallen away.

How can he know whether he'll love her forever?

*

It sniffs for a clue, but to what? It can sense the erosion in this calamitous patch of nature. It's crossed stone partitions and fields to get here. Now it scampers down a street that's crowded with tented stands, men and women selling garlands and mediaeval tomes. It can't find its way. Completely lost, its head down, it curls up under a patio table at a restaurant. A woman who's reading strokes its back. Groups of people stop to take pictures — damp with sweat, bags on their shoulders, and probably on a pilgrimage. He feels overcome with sadness here in this place where manors abound. The woman's not alone; she's with an older man. Their conversation is not a happy one.

Why did we ever come to Sarlat?

They're arguing because she hadn't wanted to come, but he'd insisted on its beauty. They fall quiet for a bit while the murmur of voices rises to a commotion — cups clanging, broken glass, foreign groups and guides, all under a greyish glow in that world of black and white. The man asks if the place brings back bad memories; he senses she must have been here before. The woman assures him that she has not. Suddenly, she lowers her voice.

The dog indulges in her attentions, but its desire to wander ripens unexpectedly. It hears a cry down the road. Someone's fallen down in the middle of the cobblestone street and cracked open their head. There's lots of blood. Everyone runs over in alarm.

It senses the anxiety, the tourists who wish to avoid

anything ill-fated. It looks up at its protectors, imploring them. Still, the couple does not rise. Men and women plod along, freighted by their heavy pasts.

The dog cowers at a familiar scent, bolting away from the nuzzling hand.

XIX

THE OLD MAN.
THE SON.
EMMA.

The old man sleeps in the armchair beside the fireplace, caught in an unsettling dream. His hands, rooted to the sides of the chair, tremble from time to time. The shooting arrow stills — threats never really come from afar. He sees his mother tending to the wash in the laundry room, beating the vast white sheets against the stone with a wooden wash stick.

It's a memory not his own, borrowed from a dream. If he were to wake, he'd find Emma just about to prepare a wild rabbit, a gift from Marianne, over a bed of potatoes roasted in garlic and turmeric. That itself would bring back the true memory of his mother, never to be seen in the laundry room. Old age prevents him from raising a bridge of words between those two realities.

All things are born and die in a moment. There are, necessarily, interruptions, opacities. He sees himself standing behind a boy who's just trampled a bird's nest. He reprimands him; he hadn't wanted to raise his voice but does. The boy glares back, hate swelling up inside of him; he's had that look in his eyes from a very young age. Words come to him from a constant radio stream: protests, cries, a gas leak in Bergerac. But it all blurs together in that border of a dream, a word suspended between two flanks. Tangled in his own lassitude, he resists waking up — to his lunch, his afternoon pill, a doctor's visit.

He thinks of the library. Weeks have passed since he last took up his work there; the thought of it gives him little pleasure. It's much too cold on November days like these, and he fears slipping on a patch of frost, even though Emma clears the path and freshens up the space, replacing the flowers and tidying up. It seems that he could go over at any moment and find everything to his liking, although from the spot he now occupies, it's as far in the distance as his childhood.

He sits up. He'll be sure to show how much he enjoys his food. As he well should: poor Emma, how boring it all must be for her.

∗

The project he's been planning to break ground on two years from now is nearly ready. He really only needs the land past the house. He'll let the rest of the property be since, after all, that part will eventually be his anyway. He'll get the permits one by one and build the complex. The only hiccup happens to be crucial, but he's already thought it out. He'll have the documents ready by the end of the week, with or without Guillaume's help. But he's fed up. He picks at his teeth and dozes off a bit with a newspaper in hand — goddamn workers, every day a new goddamn strike.

Coffee?

Claudine, that's what she'd said her name was. He'd been watching her. Her cooking is awful but she has great tits, that's for sure. That anguish rushes over him again, his mother's anguish when his father would leave for Lyon. He wipes his forehead with a handkerchief. He sees her lying in bed, a brilliant white lights him up. What a woman, really. But now he'll have Claudine. He waits. Half past two. There's no way she's getting by with what they pay her here. All the filth in the laundry room needs to be cleaned up — his goddamn father and those goddamn birds. And that damn library. All that filth. Five past three. Then ten.

Sixty euros, plus a ride?

*

She's wearing a red, jacquard jumper that she bought on a trip to Méribel during that terribly snowy winter with Olivier and Marianne, who came along since she had separated. She'd made the right choice, she looked better than ever, and they'd become close friends. If it weren't for Marianne, she wouldn't have it in her to finish a single runner, to roast a single poulard, to prepare a single confit. All of those walks, those afternoons of putting up with Michel.

This one turned out rather well, even though she doesn't know where to put it. That's how she keeps herself busy, and he could show up any moment now. He's already called three times today and there's no telling what he might do. She lifts her gaze and contemplates the walls. A portrait of a young Olivier, with such presence; Aunt Amélie's chest of drawers; the dresses she'd brought with her thirty years ago, that georgette fabric with black-and-white birds, the muslin; the silver vanity set that he'd insisted on buying in an antique shop in Paris.

It's too expensive, Olivier!

She speaks the words aloud, taken aback at the sound of her own voice. Without realising, she starts to cry and can't stop, she cries unwanted tears with a hand to her mouth so as not to wake him. How can she tell him that Michel forced her to forge his signature? That he'd threatened to shut him away in an old folks' home? That the only thing keeping her alive is the runner she's now undoing, the one she doesn't want to finish despite the constant pain in her knees, the agony of setting out the pills at exact times, the silence imposed by that second bouquet of flowers?

XX

THE LOVERS.
CÉCILE'S DOG.
THE FLORIST.

The young man's hand rests on her lap. It's broad and firm, vital. Eyes closed, he thinks he'll just stay still for a while. He wants to remember how they got here. He can vaguely make out the road in his mind, the house's façade, the library entryway, the back door to the garden, their first lunch here. The shutters and the chrysalis.

Bookcases flanked both sides of the bed, shelves uneven. If he concentrates, he can smell them. They'd picked out several volumes, read them while sitting on the shaded doorstep, feet out on the grass. She'd chosen a few excerpts and, together, they'd try to make sense of them. Bees zoomed around the verdant ash trees, the rosebush's calyces exuding their perfume. He wanted only to love her then, much like now.

He listens to her soft breathing. They would read about dying heroes and honourable lives. About stubborn cowards. One night a dreadful face had watched them from the window. But he couldn't peel himself from her arms, her pretty, copper handkerchief, the favours of stillness. Yet he can admit that, compared to then, he's now far more wary of her love. Undeserving, even. He's paralyzed by so much beauty. Still, he can remember.

In his dream, he sees a crowd of people pleading for help, but her dress is too pretty and stopping would be inconvenient. Her dress is honey and he's trapped in it. He floats his fingers above her knee. He could point at what's going on outside, but if he moves even slightly, she'll wake up. He can't bear to see the stupor in her almond eyes as she meets the depths of another gaze.

*

The dog scurries into the dark recesses of a temple. He feels compelled by a sing-song voice in the very back corner. Musicians rehearse, and there's a man dressed in a black robe with a leather strap across his chest. A mandolin hangs from it.
 . . . *maia, ni fuelhs de faia* . . .
The dog's distraught. It's been looking for answers for days, and growling isn't getting it anywhere. The musicians joke with the grey-eyed man.
Come on, Rimbaud. The world's full of women!
The man banters along with them, smiling as he sings. He notices the dog, and now they're all staring at it. He sticks out his hand and fans his fingers, his voice trilling in tandem. Then he shuts his fist as if grabbing a doorknob, lifts his fingers again and twirls his index finger. He does the same thing several times, until he stops. Now everyone's quiet. It's not going well. It's the town's sickly air. The singing man leaves.
It clamps its fangs into the hunk of bread they've tossed its way. Bread still in its mouth, it bolts, set on finding him.

*

She puts the most delicate bunches to the side so she can line up her stands and bring out the big table she uses for larger arrangements. The structure takes shape in her hands. She has to get everything done today. She focuses on braiding the blooms into the green vine with a few strings of twine, then mists it all with water and works on fastening everything securely: a few white chrysanthemums, then a few burgeoning yellows. She has to add the smallest ones with tweezers. Plenty of carnations and, in the back, ample palm leaves. When she gets to the top, she ties a silk ribbon, broad and purple, in a bow. It hangs down the middle. All that's missing is a name. She wasn't told whom it's for.

She's not quite her joyful self. This is the first funeral wreath she's made since opening up her shop: her first death. She runs through the list of older clients in her head. The town's silence presses against the shop window. She's tired. She carries the wreath and sets it on her tallest easel. What a fate for these flowers. The little bell at the door rings out desperately and she doesn't dare turn around.

It's for Claudine.

Pascal collapses into her arms, wrapping the florist in the salty cyst of death.

XXI

THE CHRYSALIS.
THE TRACKER.
THE OLD MAN.

The chrysalis must watch over the lovers — the contingent figures of this very story — detached as they may be from the profound enigma they inspire. It must prevail against the struggle of calling them together, providing for them, guarding them again and again with the same, unvarying elements, as in sestina form.

To speak of struggle one must ask: What befits poetic knowledge? What suits knowledge real and true? The lovers collect spiders from the tangle of old age and transform them into memory. They are lovers lent to time, beautiful noontide animals, shielded from inclement weather. The reader mustn't know that they aren't themselves or that everything is one and all at once. On the other hand, she should appreciate its embrace, setting her off on a long, unhurried rhythm toward a conventional reflection on the nature of the poem.

This is the essential knowledge possessed by a reader of poetry. The lovers sing of love and death to the same melody, opening themselves up to the mirror's dark reflection, bathed in their own lust. They also draw away from one another, accepting the inevitable turning of the wheel, the variance of desire. The tuned harpsichord plays alongside them, one note after the other in the doorway to another world. The man goes back to reading every now and again, accompanied by the music. He tests out a certain syntax: straightforward, concentric, sharp, artful. Sometimes unyieldingly melancholy in the hands of Pierre Hantaï.

In the marital bed, the listless bodies guide the notes that blanket them against the loneliness of the world. How to tell if it was love? The sounds refuse to blend, their heaviness rouses a part of reason while the rest plays out on the universal string, one key, then another, until it fades away.

*

Where's Cécile's dog? Where is it? The tracker navigates this crisis alone, he's scared something's happened. At Olivier's place, they told him someone died, a woman. He calls Cécile and she doesn't pick up. And the kids? He calls their grandmother and she doesn't pick up either. And the dog? He's not aware that it's been lost for weeks now. He knows the region well, has searched the forests and paths, country houses, and still nothing. It used to never leave his side. Where is it now?

He drives past the flower shop but doesn't notice it's dark inside, doesn't notice the silence, the emptiness. He makes his way across town without seeing the black hornets settling into the linden trees in the plaza; without understanding why a funeral cortege is blocking his turn or why the wreath on the hearse features several yellow flowers, though the rest of them are white. Two bees float above them. He parks like everyone else and walks into the cemetery. He doesn't notice the florist's lavender eyes or Emma's seriousness, or the tense way Pascal is carrying himself.

His life is a mess, it's all slipped from his hands, gotten

away from him. He glances at the grave without really seeing it and thinks that his own time is a black hole swarming with hornets that swallow up his energy, his life force. Falling down into the hole are the break-ups, infidelities, job contracts, pink slips, the bouquet of yellow roses, a child born much too soon, keys to all those abandoned houses, a drunk young woman pulling down his trousers, fever, the fever of survival, the delirium of hands that burn everything they touch — everything.

He suddenly turns in desperation and encounters Pascal's weary face.

Where's Cécile's dog?

And the earth falls over Claudine's coffin with the slight turn of a shovel.

∗

The old man isn't sure why he's crying. A moss of sadness shrouds the table where he's always worked. What does the word "fennel" mean, beyond the letters that comprise it? And "town"? And "white roses"? Not a single branch where he might hang his paralysing doubts. There's nothing else for him to do there.

He clasps his hands together and begins to tremble, stung by a frigid cold. And there's nothing left for him. Maybe Emma's sighs as he sleeps, his son's constant surveillance, the weight of stagnant love. No one ever told him of these humiliations, about this rosary of atonements that symbolise old age.

He tangles his fingers like vine shoots, he wants to drink the wine of bygone days, to feel bone weary.

XXII

THE LOVERS.
THE OLD MAN.
THE HORNET.

The young woman plays with her hands as if making shadow puppets, but the room's too dark to project anything at all. It's been days since she's seen the old man, though she's certainly heard him dragging things around. Sometimes it gets noisy, but they haven't felt inclined to cross the doorway.

She contemplates her lover's grey eyes, all tenderness. She wants nothing else to draw her in but this. Some days it's as if someone's lurking around the house. Other times she can only sense the brilliant sun, the fierce mountain wind. She can't remember where she's from or why she's here. All she can do is give in to the motions of love, perfecting and examining them. In the depths of the mirror, she can sense her own body. It looks ancient, subject to permanent brightness. One time, she went to a modiste in Bordeaux. She knew of a woman there — a very old one. She brought her some dresses to refashion.

They're for my honeymoon.

The woman sewed dexterously. In the small parlour where she worked, there was also a typewriter, portraits of men in caps. She must have loved so intensely. Did she miss them?

At my age, love is old hat.

The dresses were exquisite, but what she liked most was the copper-coloured scarf. The woman had cut it out from a piece of fabric that had been folded up in a trunk for years. She sewed little glass beads along the hem, so that she could take something old with her.

You'll learn that everything hurts, even the good things.

She looks at the scarf. The colour's lost its brilliance. The young man wakes and smiles before uttering a word.

*

He's had to switch a light on because it's hard to make anything out. Someone's tapping on the outside window. The old man limps toward the door. There's a tall woman, her short bob in waves, a shock of white. He doesn't seem surprised to see her.

They've known each other for so long now that their gestures are a show of familiarity. She takes a seat at one of the empty chairs around his work table, expecting him to do the same. The ride from Bordeaux has worn her out. She tells him so solemnly, the lining of her woollen, cream-coloured skirt showing as she crosses her legs. She's wearing an oversized brooch on her chest: a silver backdrop encrusted with rubies and three textured branches. Her overwhelming love for this room radiates from her lavender gaze. The messy books possess a certain charm, and the old man seems to have found respite from the lassitude that's been hounding him of late.

It's ready.

She flips through it and randomly stops at her chapter "Honey Flower." *Hors du temps*. Outside of time, the frenzied bees fill the calyx with honey. The woman's velveteen voice settles in the room like a dull film: she and the old man look like a still from the past, lost among morbid tones of sienna. They discuss the vocabulary. Then they're quiet for a while. The man knows this is his swan song, and so does she.

Don't leave without the roses.

Like always. The woman pulls out her bag and places the flowers inside. Before she leaves, she turns the snow globe. Soon it will be the dead of winter. There's a heavy road ahead. As his author makes her way down the path, the translator shuts the door and bolts it.

※

Everything's still for a moment. Under the ash trees, the beehives have shepherded in the country house's every springtime. That's how it's always been. The world shines in the secret of their overflowing honeycombs. But there's a louder buzz out there.

A massive hornet — black thorax and yellow legs — slips between the splintered wood. It doesn't go in all the way, only hovers at the edge, threateningly. The queen bee starts dying as soon as it's born. It carries not only the fatigue of death but that of the toiling bees, too, as they begin to fall ill from being trapped in the hive. Yet perhaps there's nothing to fear — it's just one insect against them all.

Soon enough, it's nightfall and there are more of them circling that satisfying protein. They feed without hunger, machine-like. There's no way out for their prey. They decapitate the bees, one at a time. One, two, three quick stings and their bodies are mangled. Soon it's all a mass of wings, legs, yellow abdomens sliced in two. A horizon of opaque bodies charred like solid smoke. There's no defence. The community is destroyed. The invader sits brazenly, extracting the soon-to-be-born and the soon-to-be-dead. It sucks on their heads, drains their juices, fills up on it all.

Not one hornet but ten, twenty, force their way in and raze thousands of bees in just a few hours. Muddled together in agony, soon it's all a mass grave. The honey spills — a waste. The victorious abandon the scene and, not far from there, they calmly build their own impenetrable nest. In the end, every dictatorship has its architects.

XXIII

EMMA.
CÉCILE'S DOG.
THE LOVERS.

The pain in her knees has only gotten worse. The boiler's been leaking for days and Guillaume can't make it over. They have to carry on there in the kitchen, where the evenings are long and Olivier goes hours without saying a word. For some time now, she's feared his condition may be deteriorating. She can't take it much longer. She throws on a coat and heads out toward the forest. She trudges up the meadow until she gets to the ash trees, then passes the ferns nestled under the pines until she reaches the stone wall separating their property from their neighbours'. She's out of breath. Her fingers claw a hole between the stones, where she then places her lips. A muffled scream.

I can't do this anymore.

She stuffs the hollow space with grass. They await her — Michel with his documents, Olivier with his silence, the house she'd made every effort to pass off as a home, the years of loneliness, the desperate hold on her friendship with Marianne. She runs down the hill without a thought to the pain, she runs to free herself of the pent-up rage of all those empty hours that slipped through her fingers in meals, table runners, nephews and nieces, newspapers. Where does it all end?

A thick fog hangs over the rooftops, nearly blotting out the edges of the church merlons. It's sure to storm. And she'll once again take pains to close the shutters and scold Olivier for not dressing warmly enough, to gather the fallen branches in front of the pergola for firewood, to preserve the figs for marmalade, can the mushrooms for confit, join the association for the protection of the bees, go shopping in Bergerac, spend quality time with Marianne, Paul and Claude, buy two bouquets in town each month and feel a lifetime full of empty hours, empty hands, an empty womb.

*

The river carries deeds unspoken in its currents. It's not too late to drag out the secrets and distresses of those characters who have settled around its waters. It moves far beyond broad stretches of plane trees and friendly shadows, touristy ports of call, larger towns and cities. It knows that, sooner or later, everything must flow downriver. All of it collects along the riverbed — the mud, the dirty pebbles, the heaviness that erosion leaves behind, the weak temperaments of some and the fickleness of others, the malice of a few. A water gushing yet still.

The mad dog barks at the realisation, exhausted. It flees from Cécile's crushing scent; from the tracker's captive smell; from the blood spilled in the streets; from the foetid stench of that madman Michel being dragged away by the police, poor Claudine; from the streaming aroma of the singing man; from the young woman, too, and her magnolia hands.

The clamour of the water, the eddies. It leaps in, gulps down river water, finds itself swept downstream, eyes tattered like the clouds.

At last, freedom.

※

So she's not obsessing over the chrysalis? The young man misinterprets her silence because she, despite it all, draws close to the windowpane on the French door and leaves behind a fleeting cloud of rosy breath near the cocoon still clinging there.

Our time's up.

He lies down tenderly and embraces her. First he kisses the lobe of her ear, then traces her lips with his, going ever so slowly, and then, turning back with the tip of his tongue, slips it into her mouth. His hands sink down to her hips, and her spine arches.

The woman observes her lover. He's like a teenager, and she can't fathom such beauty. She, on the other hand, feels the weight of the years, her wilting wings drying up. Water, she needs water. She finds a jug on the table in the library, a small plate with seeds scattered on top and a spindle with wool. She must go through with it.

She combs her hair and dons one of the dresses she once wore. But the young man wants her, and in their game he frees her from her attire. Yet she could be his mother. She reads his caress as a marvel and lets herself go. They both know that nothing is enough, that there's never enough, that each time they go to bed the lament of present love gives way to anguish in the night to come. That every word spoken slips between the sheets like a field mouse that barely shakes the grass.

XXIV

THE OLD MAN.
THE TRACKER.
THE FLORIST.

He watches throngs of people snake through darkness and shadow. The old man senses their courage. From over where there's nothing at all, he can hear them clamouring on about extinction: security, extradition, purity. They move forward: amorphous, grey, compact. From the other end, it slowly grows brighter. He can see uniforms and flickering light. He needs to figure out what to make of his cowardice. But in his dream, he can do no harm. All he can do is watch. That the lovers live to be betrayed by their own passion assuages him — they're not getting anything from it, no, and they're growing old in vain.

It's too late to be a hero. If he wasn't one then, he won't be one now, and they alert him to his own inaction. Still, once in a while he'll attempt to enlighten them about the symbolic traps of time: wars that leave millions dead, the bees' hurried escape, how we forget anyone who doesn't die in battle: better off dead than superfluously living.

Still, he can't shake off this melancholy, a melancholy that blots out the light. He's chilled to the bone. The ground's made of marble. Men and women cling to each other in the nude, trying to make love, but they fall to the snow and the cold settles over them. They cry out in pain.

White against white, like little larvae, they writhe and then die.

*

He's been called up again. The plague has spread and they need more people on the ground. For how long this time? He'll have to keep track of every detail, though they don't know when they'll be able to pay him. But never mind that — Cécile's given him another chance, and this time he doesn't want to lose her. He thinks back on his methods. He can handle it. Though the kilometres he's already travelled have laid bare the breadth of the disaster. It's too late.

He's already caught sight of several northern hornets among the trees lining the road. The plague's unstoppable. It's all moot now, though there's an order to stop circulating produce: plants, fruit, vegetables. Of course, the hornets could have hitched a ride on any old flower shipment.

He should let the florist know, but he hasn't seen her since his last visit. He's got one house left to check out before he's done: there's an old couple that never leaves and two travellers that nobody in town knows. Apparently they go at it like rabbits. People talk about them at Guillaume's bar. A man with shaking hands teeters beside a woman with a curt look on her face. Their combined years have piled up like dust in a doorway, and unevenly so.

Track all you'd like.

He checks the inside of the house: huge chimneys, a giant wooden pantry chock-full of tightly sealed jars. There's still honey there and a large table, tomatoes, wine, newspapers, medication. Bedroom, bed, portraits, restored beams. No

point in writing all this up.
What about over there?
Nothing, just the library.

The woman walks him over while the old man takes a seat. How do they manage on their own out here? They take the garden steps down to the second dwelling. She pushes the door open and walks him in. Everything is neat and tidy: a table with no books, a snow globe, chairs lined up symmetrically, empty shelves.

You've never had any plants in here?

The woman shakes her head. She doesn't want to think about the flowers that the writer from out of town takes with her when she visits. The tracker jots down notes.

Is this door unlocked?

He waits for the old woman to give him permission, but she doesn't. At first, he doesn't pick up on it, but slowly, the hiss begins to drown everything out, the rising murmur spinning into a black mass suspended above the bed. A giant sphere hangs from the central beam, an implacable army of velveteen hornets zooming in and out. It's unstoppable. He shatters the windows and frantically starts driving them out. Fucking hell.

The tracker flaps his arms in a frenzy until there's nothing left in the room but shadow. He switches on the light. He gapes at the sphere in horror. It's bigger than he'd thought. Thousands. Clearly shaken, the tracker hurries out to make a call.

Hours go by, and Emma is paralyzed on the other side of the doorway. Olivier, in a state, is alone in the house, clasping his hands together to still a shake he's never felt before. Men storm into the house well into the night, carrying two body bags. They extract the naked bodies from the infested room.

They're elderly.

No one knows who they are or where they're from. A gauzy, beaded scarf mercifully hides their faces.

∗

She's stuck in traffic. The motorway to Bordeaux is jam packed. Significant delays. On the radio, the authorities ask that everyone keep calm and stay home so that the plague won't spread any further. Bees aren't their only target anymore. Groups of more than three are banned, as is watering plants, filling up pools, parties and gatherings. Strangely enough, the species has survived the winter. The florist slams off her radio. She's made up her mind to deliver this final order.

She's visiting an aunt who's fallen ill in the city. She makes it past the checkpoints. In her luggage, fastened with purple ribbon, one last bunch of roses for the woman with the white hair.

point in writing all this up.
What about over there?
Nothing, just the library.

The woman walks him over while the old man takes a seat. How do they manage on their own out here? They take the garden steps down to the second dwelling. She pushes the door open and walks him in. Everything is neat and tidy: a table with no books, a snow globe, chairs lined up symmetrically, empty shelves.

You've never had any plants in here?

The woman shakes her head. She doesn't want to think about the flowers that the writer from out of town takes with her when she visits. The tracker jots down notes.

Is this door unlocked?

He waits for the old woman to give him permission, but she doesn't. At first, he doesn't pick up on it, but slowly, the hiss begins to drown everything out, the rising murmur spinning into a black mass suspended above the bed. A giant sphere hangs from the central beam, an implacable army of velveteen hornets zooming in and out. It's unstoppable. He shatters the windows and frantically starts driving them out. Fucking hell.

The tracker flaps his arms in a frenzy until there's nothing left in the room but shadow. He switches on the light. He gapes at the sphere in horror. It's bigger than he'd thought. Thousands. Clearly shaken, the tracker hurries out to make a call.

Hours go by, and Emma is paralyzed on the other side of the doorway. Olivier, in a state, is alone in the house, clasping his hands together to still a shake he's never felt before. Men storm into the house well into the night, carrying two body bags. They extract the naked bodies from the infested room.

They're elderly.

No one knows who they are or where they're from. A gauzy, beaded scarf mercifully hides their faces.

※

She's stuck in traffic. The motorway to Bordeaux is jam packed. Significant delays. On the radio, the authorities ask that everyone keep calm and stay home so that the plague won't spread any further. Bees aren't their only target anymore. Groups of more than three are banned, as is watering plants, filling up pools, parties and gatherings. Strangely enough, the species has survived the winter. The florist slams off her radio. She's made up her mind to deliver this final order.

She's visiting an aunt who's fallen ill in the city. She makes it past the checkpoints. In her luggage, fastened with purple ribbon, one last bunch of roses for the woman with the white hair.

XXV

EMMA.

The fig tree won't survive the winter. Two of its branches have withered and the trunk is in bad shape. Tourism's on the decline. It'll take years for things to blow over. Emma walks out to the garden, a scarf around her shoulders. She's tired. She contemplates the solitude of the countryside, the vacant path. Michel failed to secure his permits; he won't be bothering them any time soon. She won't say anything to Olivier about Claudine.

She goes back into the house to make coffee. She puts the water on to boil and adds two heaping tablespoons, then lets it steep before filtering out the grounds. She pours it into a large mug, adds plenty of sugar, too, then turns on the television. A cooking show is on. She grabs a pen and paper. It's finally come to her: a better way to make Lyonnaise duck and pastry, for when her nieces and nephews come to visit. She sips the final dregs. She has chores lined up for the morning, readying the bedroom and changing the sheets. They've given the walls a fresh coat of paint and hung up huge prints of Parisian views.

She smiles as a tear streams down her face. She's smiling because she still has life left to live. She slowly makes her way down to the garden. They'd aired the bedroom out, put most of the books in boxes, ready to be sold, and got rid of the mirror. They'd slept here way back when they were renovating the house. The best of times. Then they'd turned it into a guest room. She wipes things down, tidies up. She locks the library door behind her.

It's no longer necessary.

It's getting late. She must make Olivier breakfast and bring it to him in bed. The room is quiet. The morning sun rises, cast in meagre colours and heavy clouds. His bed, topped with a green comforter, faces the garden. From there he can spy the windows, the guest room's old shutter door, a threshold he hadn't crossed since they'd carried out those old, weightless bodies. She remembers it with a sigh of relief.

A blizzardwind rushes against the doorframe to the outside world. At first just barely, then thunderously. It's the only sound. An intense blackness has spread up the white wood, a blackness that creeps. But the note tacked onto the beam is dirty and impossible to read. The scent of damp willows and ash trees — of a forest drowned in sorrow — travels on the wind.

The chrysalis has nothing in its charge; it relinquishes such hardship. Powerless, it finds release and falls to the ground. The first frost is on its way. Imperceptibly at first, then steadily, the snowflakes storm what remains open, blanketing the cocoon and covering the footprints of those final gravediggers in a soft layer of white ash.

Another spring may never come.

Où, avec des éperons de genièvre,
pousses-tu
la bête de midi, une bête prêtée?
— Paul Celan